W9-BNQ-424

My name is Roger.

What is your
name? _____

New Kid on the Block

Jennifer Moore-Mallinos
Illustrations: Marta Fàbrega

WE ARE LEAVING!

When Mom and Dad first told me that we
were moving, I didn't want to believe them.
Why would they want to take us to a new place,
far away, where we wouldn't know anybody?
I thought that maybe they were teasing me,
but then, when the day arrived and a moving
truck pulled into our driveway, I knew for sure
that it was true. There was no turning back
now, we were leaving!

WHAT ABOUT MY FRIENDS?

The reason was Dad's job. He said he had to work at a new place that was six hours away from our home, and that's why we had to move.

Well, Dad may have been excited about moving to his new office, but I was sad. What if all my friends forget about me and what if my new teacher doesn't like me? I was scared about a lot of things because I had never moved before…but part of me was a little bit excited too!

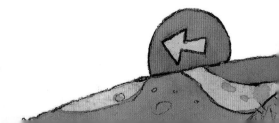

GOOD-BYE TO EVERYONE

After the moving truck was all loaded, Mom, Dad, and I held hands and walked around our empty house one last time. I thought about all the great times we had had in our house. I sure was going to miss it! Later, I said good-bye to all my friends and we promised each other that we would call or write. The hardest part though, was when we got in the car and drove away. I tried hard not to cry but I couldn't help it; even Mom shed a few tears. It was sad for all of us!

MAYBE IT WON'T BE SO BAD...

Just like Dad said, it took six hours to drive to our new house. By the time we finally got there, I was feeling a bit better. In fact, I already had some big plans for my new bedroom. As soon as Dad parked the car, I looked around. Across the street I saw some kids playing catch. One of them stopped and waved, so I smiled and waved back. Maybe this won't be as bad as I thought it would be.

A LOT OF THINGS TO UNPACK

The first few days in our new house were spent unpacking millions and millions of boxes and putting things away. There were so many boxes that by the time Monday came and I had to go to school, I was glad. I don't think I could have unpacked or even looked at another box!

FIRST CONTACT WITH THE SCHOOL

On my first day of school I was allowed to go in before the bell rang so that my principal could show me how to get to my class. My school seemed kind of nice.

The hallways were filled with bright colors and there were paintings and special projects hanging on the walls outside the classrooms. My classroom was upstairs, at the end of the corridor.

NEW TEACHER, NEW CLASSROOM

When I got to my class, my teacher, Mrs. Henry, was waiting for me at the door. She shook my hand and invited me into the classroom. While Mrs. Henry was showing me around the room, the bell rang for all the kids to come in. That's when I got kind of scared. Mrs. Henry quickly showed me which desk was mine and then went to greet the kids.

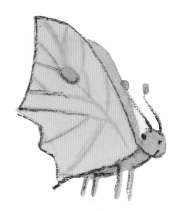

MY NEIGHBOR IS ALSO HERE!

While I checked out my desk, the classroom started to fill up with kids so I pretended to be busy. I didn't want anybody to see that I was nervous.
I was even hoping that nobody would notice me, but they did. One kid with fluffy brown hair came up to my desk and said "Hey, you must be the new kid on the block." I realized that he was the same kid who had waved at me from across the street the day we moved in.
His name was Vince.

VINCE AND HIS FRIENDS

My first day of school wasn't so bad.
Vince and I ate lunch together and
we hung out at recess. Vince showed
me around the playground and I met
some of Vince's other friends.
Everybody was really nice. Vince told
me that he knew what it was like
to be the new kid on the block and
he wanted to help me out. I was glad!

GETTING USED TO SO MANY THINGS...

It took me a while to find my way around the school and it was hard getting used to my new house, but things were getting better. Now, some of the other kids in my neighborhood and I walk to school together and sometimes we ride our bikes instead. Then after school, when I've finished my homework, we all hang out together and play catch or street hockey. It's a lot of fun!

I STILL KEEP MY OLD FRIENDS

I'm glad that I have some new friends now, but I still miss my old friends. The other day, when Mom let me call a few of my old friends, I told them about my new house and my new school and I told them about Vince and some of the other kids. And the weird part was that even though I was talking to them over the phone, it seemed like old times again and didn't feel like I had ever left. We were all still friends!

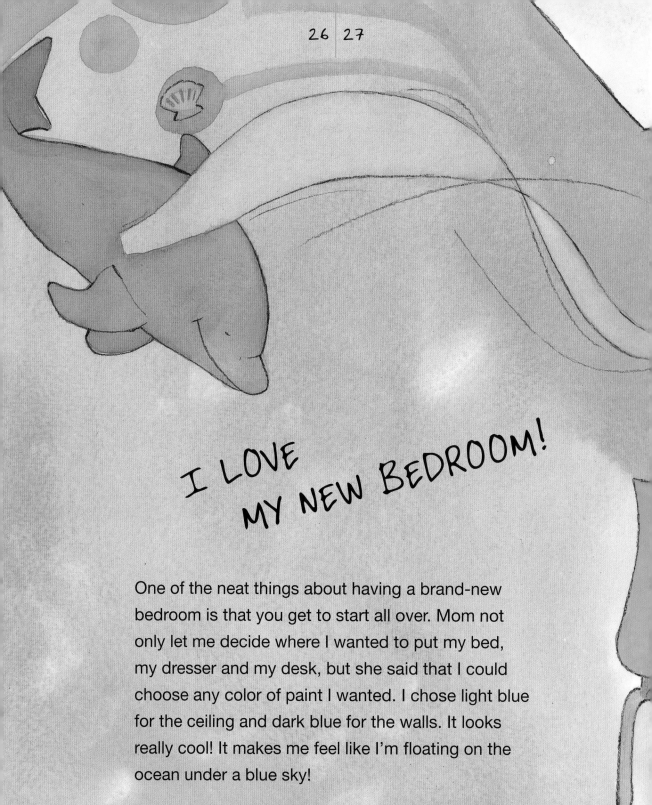

I LOVE MY NEW BEDROOM!

One of the neat things about having a brand-new bedroom is that you get to start all over. Mom not only let me decide where I wanted to put my bed, my dresser and my desk, but she said that I could choose any color of paint I wanted. I chose light blue for the ceiling and dark blue for the walls. It looks really cool! It makes me feel like I'm floating on the ocean under a blue sky!

SOME THINGS WILL NEVER CHANGE...

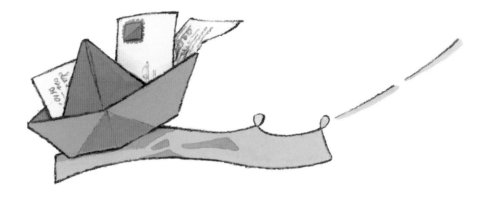

It's funny how many things change
when you move and how many things
stay the same. I have a new house,
new school and new friends, but
Mom and Dad are the same and
they make me do the same chores
around the house.
Mom said that in the summer we
can go to visit my old friends. That
will be awesome!

JUST HAVE
CONFIDENCE!

So, if you ever end up being the new kid on the block
like I did, don't worry! Just have confidence in yourself
and trust your parents! Before you know it, you'll make
new friends, join new teams, and then the next thing
you know, somebody else will become the new kid
on the block.

Activities

DECISION DICE

New friendships are always exciting and fun because everything you do together is new. However, deciding how you want to spend your time together can sometimes be awkward and even difficult. Are you a bit shy about saying what you want to do?

Then, why not roll the dice and let them decide for you!

This is how you can make a die together with a new friend:

Get cardboard, some glue or tape, marker pens, and scissors. The drawing shows how to make a six-sided die. Write an activity on each side and then put it together and glue or tape it.

You may want to make additional dice in order to have a lot of activities to choose from.

Have fun and roll away!

FIND-A-FRIEND ADDRESS BOX/BOOK

For many of us who have moved to a new home in a new neighborhood, keeping in touch with friends and family is very important. Whether you call a friend on the phone or write an e-mail message, keeping track of all this information can be hard.

So let's make keeping in touch a lot easier by putting all of our friends' and family's information in one place! To make your very own "Find-a-Friend" address box or book you will need a shoebox or scrapbook, cue cards or lined paper, scissors, glue, marker pens, crayons, stickers, beads (optional), stickers and glitter glue.

Decorating your address box or book can be a lot of fun. Make your box or book as fancy as you want. Draw pictures, make designs, add glitter and use photos of your friends and family to decorate the box. Keep adding new information as you make new friends!

BICYCLE WASH DAY

Everybody likes to have a squeaky clean bike! And you would like to meet new kids in your neighborhood. So a bike wash would be a great idea!

First get your parents' permission. Then you'll need to make some posters. Get a few large pieces of cardboard and write a short message inviting the kids in your neighborhood to the first annual bike wash. Make sure that you include the date of your bike wash, where the bike wash will take place, and ask them to bring their sponges and bikes for an afternoon of fun in the sun! Hang your posters around the neighborhood where people will see them.

On the day of the bike wash, make sure that you have buckets full of soapy water and that there is clean water available for rinsing the soap off the bikes. Provide towels for drying the bikes.

Some other ideas to make your bike wash a success: Play music, provide refreshments and make sure that you learn at least three new names of the kids attending. Have fun, make new friends and scrub hard!

POSTCARD CREATIONS

Everybody loves receiving a postcard in the mail! Whether you send a postcard to a new friend or an old friend, it's a great way to keep in touch and to let others know how you are doing and that you are thinking of them. So let's make our very own postcard and stay in touch with those we like!

To make your postcard, cut a 3 x 5 inch (rectangular) piece of white cardboard. Postcards are two sided: On one side is a picture. For example, if you have a friend who loves dogs, you might want to draw a picture of a dog or even cut out a picture of a cute fluffy puppy from a magazine and stick it on your postcard. Or maybe you want to show your friend a picture of your new house by either drawing it or gluing a photo of your house to the postcard. Make it colorful and fun!

The other side of the postcard is divided in half. On the left side of the postcard, you write your message to your friend and on the other side, you write his or her address. And remember to make sure that you place a stamp on the top right hand side just above the address!

Parent's guide

Moving from one community or country to another is a familiar experience for many children and their families. Whether a move is initiated by a family's finances or for work-related opportunities, every family's decision to move is unique to their individual situation. However, despite these differences, many children share similar feelings and concerns toward the concept of moving.

NEW KID ON THE BLOCK identifies some of the feelings and concerns. It acknowledges that moving can be an emotional experience for the whole family and also recognizes the need for children to maintain a sense of stability. Many things change when a family moves, such as communities and neighborhoods, friends and schools, but some of the most important things, such as family relationships and each person's place within the family unit, remain the same.

This book is a great tool to initiate communication between you and your children. Providing them with the opportunity to talk about their feelings regarding moving, whether good or bad, may help make the transition from one place to another smoother and less traumatic.

Moving can create a wide range of emotions, from uncertainty and anxiety to excitement and a sense of adventure. Although there is often a mixture of conflicting feelings associated with moving, it is helpful for everybody, especially children, if the entire process is embarked upon in a positive way. The approach of being optimistic can have a significant and constructive impact on your child's reaction to your family's move.

Some suggestions that may help make the transition of moving a little less stressful for the children in your family:

- Inform your children as soon as possible that the family is moving. This way, your children will have time to assimilate the news and get used to the idea of moving before the actual moving day arrives.

- Affirming that your family will be together but will be living in a different house may help alleviate any anxiety your children may be feeling, while reinforcing a sense of stability during this time of change.

- Most children's initial response to the idea of moving is one of resistance. Some children may even express anger toward their parents for "making them move." Acknowledge your children's response to the news that you are moving, be patient, show the situation in a positive light, and they will come around.

- Stay positive and be enthusiastic about moving. Welcome the change by focusing on how exciting it is going to be to have a new house, a new bedroom, and all the new friends that your children will make. Make it sound exciting!

- If possible, involve your children in the process of finding a new house. Otherwise, consider showing them a picture of your new home before you arrive. This will help ease some of the stress and fear of the unknown that your children may be experiencing. You can also take some additional pictures of your children's new school and surrounding community. Most of their concerns linked to the unknown will effectively be lessened.

- When the moving day arrives, give your children the time they need to say good-bye to their home and friends. Encourage them to obtain their friends' telephone numbers, e-mail addresses and home addresses, in order to maintain contact.

- Once you have moved into your new home, if appropriate, give your children the opportunity to take part in decorating their new bedrooms. Whatever they can do to make their bedrooms their very own, will help make their transition smoother and impart a sense of belonging to their new surroundings.

Feeling scared and apprehensive about moving your family to a new home is to be expected. So try not to be too hard on yourself if *you* experience these and other similar feelings. The way you approach moving change can make a world of difference for the whole family.

New Kid on the Block

First edition for the United States and Canada
published in 2009 by Barron's Educational Series,
Inc.
© Copyright 2008 by Gemser Publications S.L.
El Castell, 38; Teià (08329) Barcelona, Spain (World
Rights)
Title of the original in Spanish: *El nuevo niño del
barrio*
Phone: 93 540 13 53
E-mail: info@mercedesros.com
Author: Jennifer Moore-Mallinos
Illustrator: Marta Fàbrega

All inquiries should be addressed to:
Barron's Educational Series, Inc.
250 Wireless Boulevard
Hauppauge, New York 11788
http://www.barronseduc.com

ISBN-13: 978-0-7641-4181-2
ISBN-10: 0-7641-4181-3

Library of Congress Control Number: 2008938296

Printed in China
9 8 7 6 5 4 3 2 1